For more than forty years,
Yearling has been the leading name
in classic and award-winning literature
for young readers.

Yearling books feature children's
favorite authors and characters,
providing dynamic stories of adventure,
humor, history, mystery, and fantasy.

Trust Yearling paperbacks to entertain,
inspire, and promote the love of reading
in all children.

OTHER YEARLING BOOKS YOU WILL ENJOY

DICK KING-SMITH

THE
WATER HORSE

Illustrated by David Parkins

A YEARLING BOOK

Visit us on the Web! www.randomhouse.com/kids

Educators and librarians, for a variety of teaching tools, visit us at
www.randomhouse.com/teachers

CONTENTS

1

An Old Fish's Egg

IT WAS KIRSTIE who found it. It was lying just above the high-tide mark, a squarish package-shaped object, the color of seaweed, with a long tendril sticking out from each of its four corners.

It was exactly the shape, in fact, of the mermaids' purses, the little horny egg capsules of the dogfish, that were commonly washed up on the beach. But this one was the size of a large cookie tin!

"Look what I've found!" shouted Kirstie. "Quick, come and look!"

In the small hours of March the 26th, 1930, a great storm struck the west coast of

Scotland. The huge seas that it had whipped up smashed against the foot of the cliffs, and the tigerish tempest ran up the face of them and grabbed a small white house on the cliff top in its jaws.

The house quivered and shook in the teeth of the wind, and Kirstie, waking in sudden fright, was sure that the roof would fly away.

The noise of the storm was fearful. Angus will be terrified, thought Kirstie, and she jumped out of bed and ran to her little brother's room next door. Her mother arrived at the same moment carrying an oil lamp, and by its light they could see that Angus was sleeping peacefully, sleeping like the baby he had been only a few years before. Outside, the thunder banged and the lightning flashed, the wind roared and the rain poured. Angus snored.

"Back to bed, Kirstie," said her mother. "I'll stay here awhile in case he wakes."

"What about Grumble?" said Kirstie. "Is he all right?"

Grumble was Mother's father, who lived
with them. When Kirstie was very small,
she had heard Mother say angrily to him
one day, "All you ever do is grumble,

grumble," and so she had thought that it was his name. It suited him. He came stumping along the corridor now, a big old man with a thick droopy mustache.

"Can't sleep a wink!" growled Grumble to his daughter and granddaughter, as though it were their fault. "Terrible weather! The Lord help sailors on a night like this!"

Kirstie and Mother grinned at one another, for Kirstie's father was a sailor, a merchant seaman. But at that moment his ship was, they knew, in quiet tropical waters, far from tonight's frenzied Atlantic storm. At that moment there came a clap of thunder so close and so loud that Angus awoke and sat up in bed.

"I heard a noise," he said in a matter-of-fact voice.

"It's a storm, Angus," said Kirstie. "A big storm."

"Going to blow the house down in a minute, I shouldn't be surprised," said Grumble.

Just for a moment the wind dropped a little, and they could all clearly hear the crash of the breakers on the beach below. What would the sea throw up? Kirstie wondered. What would they find on the shoreline tomorrow? All of them loved beachcombing, even Grumble, though he pretended he didn't, and a storm like this would leave lots of driftwood for them to collect.

"Back to sleep, everyone," Mother said, "and in the morning we'll all go down and see what we can find."

"What d'you mean—in the morning?" said Grumble. "It's morning now. *I* shan't be able to drop off again, that's for sure."

"You should count some sheep, Grumble," said Angus. "That's what I do."

"You can only count to ten," Kirstie said.

"I know. When I get to ten, I start again," said Angus firmly, and he lay down and shut his eyes.

Back in bed, Kirstie lay listening to the

roar of the storm. She was as wide awake, she felt, as it was possible to be. And then— quite suddenly, it seemed—it was broad daylight.

Kirstie was too excited to eat much breakfast. The worst of the storm had passed now, the wind had dropped a bit, and Mother had promised that they would go down to the beach as soon as breakfast was finished and the dishes were washed up. It was the thought of what might be washed up on the shore that was exciting Kirstie. Beachcombing was such fun. You never knew what you might find. There were always lots of seaweed, and creatures like starfish and jellyfish and sea urchins, and loads of shells—whelks and cockles and cowries and razor shells. Then there was trash, ·like empty bottles (perhaps one might have a message in it from a castaway), and of course there was driftwood: wooden boxes and crates, planks and spars (once, even, a pair of oars), and the strange twisted shapes of branches and sometimes quite large limbs of trees, worn pale and smooth during their long voyages from goodness knows where. With such a storm as last night's, who knows what they might find!

"Eat up, Kirstie," Mother said.

Angus never needed to be given this order. Meals, in his view, were times for eating, not for talking. From sitting up at the table to getting down from it again, he only opened his mouth to put food in it.

"What d'you think we'll find, Angus?" said Kirstie. Angus stared at her, his jaws chomping rhythmically. He did not answer.

"Aren't you excited?" Kirstie asked. Angus nodded placidly.

"My egg's not boiled enough," said Grumble.

They set out at last down the cliff path, Kirstie leading, carrying a little sack for putting things in, Mother following, holding Angus by the hand, and Grumble stumping along behind with a big sack and a length of cord to tie up bundles of drift-wood. The seas were running very strongly still, and the breakers were huge but distant now, for the spring tide had ebbed. The pebbly beach was, as always, empty of people. The only living things on it were two seagulls picking at something that lay just above the high-tide mark. They flew up as Kirstie ran forward.

"Come and look!" she shouted. "Quick!"

"What is it?" Mother shouted back.

"I don't know. It looks like a giant mermaid's purse!"

Angus ran as fast as his short legs would allow. He looked critically at the object. The gulls could not have been at it long, for it seemed unharmed.

"I didn't know there were giant mermaids," said Angus.

"No dogfish could produce a thing like that," said Mother when she and Grumble arrived. "Why, it must be twenty times as big as an ordinary mermaid's purse. What do you think, Dad? Could it have come from some huge creature, like a basking shark?"

"Don't ask me," said Grumble. "We're here to collect firewood, so let's get on with it. This cold wind gets right in my bones." He prodded the thing with his

foot. "Whatever it is, it's no use to us," he said, and he stumped on, with Mother following.

"It moved!" Kirstie said.

"'Course it did," said Angus. "Grumble kicked it."

"No, I mean after he'd kicked it—I saw the outside of it, the skin of it, move, I'm almost sure I did. It sort of trembled."

Angus peered at the giant mermaid's purse. "It isn't trembling now," he said. "'Spect it's dead. 'Spect he killed it." He looked up at his sister and saw that she was upset at this thought. "It's only an old fish's egg," he said. "Eggs don't feel anything. Those ones that Mother boiled for breakfast, they didn't feel nothing."

"They didn't feel *anything*," said Kirstie.

Angus sighed. "I just told you that," he said. "Sometimes I feel much older than you."

"Well, you're not," said Kirstie quite sharply. "You're three years younger. Hold my sack open for me." She bent down and picked up the thing. It was heavy, as heavy indeed as a large cookie tin full of cookies.

"You're not going to take it home?" said Angus.

"I am."

"Where you going to put it, then?"

"In a bucket of water. Just in case it's alive. It might hatch—you never know."

"Mother won't like it."

"Mother won't know."

"She'll ask what's in your sack."

Kirstie thought quickly. "Seaweed," she said. "Grumble puts it on the garden for manure." And on top of the thing she placed some bunches of kelp.

When they had all climbed the cliff path again—Grumble complaining loudly of the weight of the driftwood bundle he carried—the children went off together to the garden, a small plot on the sheltered side of the white cliff-top house. Here their grandfather grew vegetables, grumbling endlessly about the poorness of the soil, the unkindness of the weather, and the damage done to his plants by birds and slugs and caterpillars.

Kirstie put the seaweed on his compost heap, filled a large bucket with water, and tipped the giant mermaid's purse into it. It was too big to submerge, and two of its four tendrils stuck out forlornly above the surface.

"It's too big," Angus said.

"I can see that, silly," said Kirstie. "But at least it will keep it from drying out."

"What's it matter if it's dead anyway?"

"We don't *know* it's dead."

"Well, it soon will be."

"Why?"

Angus sighed. "It came out of the sea, didn't it? That's tap water. It needs salt water."

"Angus!" cried Kirstie. She gave him a hug. "You're brilliant!" she said.

"I know."

Making sure that Mother was else-where, Kirstie got the container of salt from the pantry and poured a generous measure into the bucket. She looked carefully at the sticking-out tendrils, but they didn't move. "It needs a bigger place," she said. "I know! The bathtub!"

How the rest of that day dragged, but at the end of it luck was on their side. Mother had had a bath after her morning's work. Grumble, on being asked, said no, he didn't want a bath, too much washing was bad for your skin, and anyway the water was always either too hot or too cold. So that only left the children. Mother gave Angus his bath at bedtime and left the water in it for Kirstie.

"He wasn't all that dirty," she said, and she took Angus downstairs to dry him by the fire, where Grumble sat listening to the radio (turned up very loud, for he was rather deaf) and moaning that the program was rubbish.

Kirstie moved fast.

First she let out Angus's bathwater. Then she put the plug back in, turned on the cold tap, and tiptoed down the stairs and out into the garden. In a couple of minutes she was back in the bathroom, the giant mermaid's purse in both hands, the container of salt tucked under one arm. She lowered her burden gently into the water, added a little hot for luck, poured the whole contents of the salt container in, turned off the taps, and went out of the bathroom, closing the door.

Kirstie awoke once in the middle of the night and could not resist opening the bathroom door and peeping in, but the thing was just floating, motionless. "You're stupid," she said to herself as she was drifting back to sleep again. "It's probably just a piece of seaweed, that's all. First thing in the morning, before anyone's up, I'll take it out and chuck it on Grumble's compost heap."

First thing in the morning, Kirstie went quietly along to the bathroom. She had just grasped the handle of the door when she thought she heard something. She bent down, her ear to the keyhole.

Through it she could hear a small splashing, such as a little fish might make breaking the surface of a stream, and then a small squeaking noise, a kind of chirrup, such as a little bird might make breaking from the shell of its egg.

Kirstie opened the bathroom door.

2

It's a Monster

ONE LOOK INTO the bathtub was enough to send her hurrying to get Angus. As usual, he awoke from the deepest of sleeps with his mind instantly tuned to his chief pleasure in life.

"I'm hungry," said Angus. "Is breakfast ready?"

"Ssssshh!" said Kirstie. "Don't talk so loud. We mustn't wake Mother or Grumble."

"Why not?"

"Because it's hatched. The thing. In the bathtub."

"Blow me down!" said Angus.

Angus enjoyed using what he thought to be terrible swear words, and his father, on his last shore leave, had taught him a careful selection of sailors' oaths.

They crept into the bathroom and stood side by side, gazing into the water.

"Look!" said Kirstie.

"Shiver my timbers!" said Angus.

The giant mermaid's purse lay on the bottom at the plug hole end like a sunken wreck. Wrecked it was, too, with a gaping hole in one side where something had emerged. At the other end of the bathtub swam that something.

When Kirstie was a grown woman with a family of her own, her children would ask her time and again to describe what it was that she saw in the bathtub that early March morning when she was eight years of age.

"It was a little animal," she told them, "such as neither I nor your Uncle Angus had ever seen before. Such as no one in the world had ever seen before, in fact. In size, it was about as big as a newborn kitten but quite a different shape. The first thing you noticed about it was its head, which was sticking out of the water on the end of quite a long neck. More than anything, it looked like a horse's head, with wide nostrils like a horse and even a suggestion of pricked ears. But its body was more like a turtle's. I don't mean it had a shell—it had

a kind of warty skin like a toad's, greeny grayish in color—but it had four flippers like a turtle has. And then it had a tail like a crocodile's. But just like you usually look at people's faces before you notice anything else about them, the thing that struck us was the look of its head. We didn't think about a crocodile or a toad or a turtle. We thought about a little horse."

Now, as Kirstie and Angus watched, the creature, which had been eyeing them in silence, dived with a plop, swam underwater with strong strokes of its little flippers, and surfaced again right in front of them. It looked up at them and chirruped.

"What does it want?" Kirstie said. The answer to this question was obvious to someone like Angus.

"Food, of course," he said. "It's hungry, like me."

"What shall we give it? What do you suppose it will eat? What do you suppose it is anyway? We don't even know what sort of animal it is."

"It's a monster," said Angus confidently. He had a number of picture books about monsters, and obviously this was one of them.

"But monsters are big," Kirstie said.

Angus sighed. "This isn't a *monster* monster," he said. "This is a baby one."

"A baby sea monster!" said Kirstie. "Well, then, it would eat fish, wouldn't it? We'll have to catch some fish for it."

A happy smile lit up Angus's round face. "We don't need to," he said. "There's some sardines in the pantry. I like sardines."

Opening the sardine can was difficult, but Kirstie managed to turn the key far enough to winkle one out, and they tiptoed upstairs again, carrying it on a saucer.

"Don't give it everything. It might not like it," said Angus hopefully, but when Kirstie pulled off a bit of sardine with her fingers and dropped it into the bathtub, the little animal snapped it up and gulped it down and chirruped loudly for more.

"It likes it," said Angus dolefully. He broke off another piece of the fish, his hand moving automatically toward his mouth, but Kirstie said "Angus!" sharply, so he dropped it in the tub, contenting himself with licking the oil off his fingers. And, one after the other, they fed the creature the rest of the sardine. Then they went down to the pantry again to see if they could get another one out of the can.

With great effort, for the key was very stiff to turn, Kirstie had at last got the can fully open when suddenly they heard footsteps on the stairs and Mother came into the kitchen.

"Kirstie!" she said. "Whatever are you up to? Who told you you could help yourself to sardines—and long before breakfast time, too?"

"It's for our sea monster," said Angus.

"Don't be so silly, Angus!" said Mother sharply. "Look at your fingers, all oily, you greedy little boy! And you, Kirstie, you're old enough to know better!"

"We haven't eaten any, Mother, honestly," said Kirstie. "And we *have* got a sea monster, truly we have."

"Now you listen to me, Kirstie," said Mother. "Whatever it is that you two have brought home—a lobster, a crab, whatever it is that you're wasting my expensive sardines on—you will take it straight back, d'you hear me?"

"Oh, no, Mother!" cried Kirstie. "Please not."

"First thing after breakfast it goes back in the sea," said Mother firmly. "Where is it anyway?"

"In the bathtub," said Angus.

"In the bathtub!" cried Mother. "Oh, no!"

"It's quite happy there," said Angus.

"Well, that's more than your grandfather will be by now. As I came down, I saw him going along the corridor with his towel and his shaving kit. He'll have a fit!"

"Specially if it's still hungry," said Angus.

But when the three of them reached the bathroom, the door was open and there was Grumble kneeling by the bathtub. With his bald head and his droopy mustache he looked like a walrus about to take a dip. He was staring silently at the little animal as it paddled around in the water, now glistening with sardine oil. To their amazement they saw that he was smiling broadly. Grumble, smiling!

"It's that thing you found on the beach after the storm, isn't it, Kirstie?"

"Yes, Grumble. It hatched in the night."

"I made her put salt in the water," said Angus.

"I doubt you need have bothered with that," said Grumble. "It's an air-breathing beastie, you see, like a seal. Fresh water or salt, I doubt it matters, so long as it has plenty of fish to eat."

"We've given it a sardine," said Kirstie.

Grumble got to his feet. "You've a clever couple of kids here," he said to Mother. "How I wish I could have found such a thing when I was their age. There were many stories then of this creature and I believed all of them, but I never thought I'd see one."

"You sound as though you know what this thing is," said Mother.

"I should," said Grumble. "Wasn't I born and brought up on the banks of Loch Morar? And wasn't there supposed to be one of these living in that very loch?"

"What is it, Grumble?" asked Kirstie.

"Before I tell you," said Grumble, "you must promise faithfully to tell no one outside the family. Not a word to any of your friends at school. Understand?"

"Oh, yes," said Kirstie. "Cross my heart." She crossed it. Angus crossed his stomach, perhaps by mistake, but possibly because it was to him the most important organ.

"Right," said Grumble. "Then I'll tell you. It's a monster."

"I told you," said Angus.

"Always there've been tales of sightings of such a beastie, sometimes at sea, more often in a loch," said Grumble. "Oh, when I was a boy, how I longed to see the kelpie."

"Is that what it's called?" said Kirstie.

"That's one name for it," said Grumble, "but the other is the one that I like. Most folk call it the Water Horse."

3

Crusoe

"THE WATER HORSE!" breathed Kirstie.

"Well, I'll be scuppered!" said Angus.

"I don't care what it is," said Mother. "It's not staying in my bathtub. I'm going to get the breakfast now and as soon as you've eaten it, that thing goes—out of the bathtub, out of this house, I don't care what you do with it. Is that understood?" And off she went. Kirstie and Angus looked so woebegone that Grumble put an arm around each of them.

"Cheer up," he said. "We'll think of some way to make sure he's all right."

"How d'you know it's a he?" said Kirstie. "It might be a she."

"That's true," said Grumble. "I don't know how you could tell. But we'll have to decide, one way or another."

"Why?" said Angus.

"So that we can give it a name. It must have a name if we're going to keep it."

"Keep it?" cried the children. "But Mother just said..."

"Your mother only said it must go out of the house. 'I don't care what you do with it'—that's what she said. So we'll decide what we want to do and then we'll do it. Now go to my room, Kirstie, and you'll see some loose change on top of the dresser. Bring me a coin—any coin will do."

When Kirstie came back with a sixpence, Grumble balanced it on his thumbnail.

"Now," he said, "heads it's a boy, tails it's a girl. All right?" and when the children nodded, he flicked the coin high in the air. It fell on its edge and rolled underneath the claw-footed bathtub. Angus, the smallest, crawled on his tummy to retrieve it.

"What is it?" asked Kirstie.

"It's a boy!" called Angus triumphantly.

"What shall we call him then?" said Grumble.

Between them, in the next few minutes, they managed to suggest a host of names, but no one approved of anyone else's choices. Kirstie liked the kind of names that might have suited a real horse or pony—

Starlight, Bonnieboy, Surefoot, Trusty, and Thunderer. Grumble favored good Scottish family names such as Stuart and Sinclair, Mackenzie, McGregor, and Tullibane. Angus chose fierce, aggressive names suitable for the enormous monster that he thought the creature would one day be, names like Skullcruncher, Superjaws, Backbreaker, Cowkiller, and Drinkblood. But they could not agree, and when Mother called that breakfast was ready, they all went to get dressed, leaving the infant Water Horse paddling namelessly around the bathtub.

Breakfast was an unusually silent meal at first. Grumble, Kirstie, and Angus were all still busy trying to think of a name. Mother was feeling a little guilty that she had reacted so harshly in ordering the immediate expulsion of the animal. After all, whatever it was, it was certainly quite extraordinary, and the children were so thrilled about it; and as for her father, why, she hadn't seen him look so happy in years. There he was now, eating his breakfast without a word of complaint. Usually the porridge wasn't salty enough, or the egg wasn't done, the toast was too light or too dark, or the tea too weak or too strong. She caught his eye and he actually winked at her.

"All right," said Mother. "I've changed my mind. You can have the rest of the day to decide among the three of you what you're going to do with the creature. But I want it out of the house by this evening. And that's my last word."

"A good decision," said Grumble.

The children beamed. Mother was encouraged to go further. "And I suppose you might as well feed it the rest of that can of sardines," she said.

"Can't I have them?" said Angus.

"No."

"A good decision," said Kirstie.

"We've been trying to think of a name for him," said Grumble.

"It's a boy," said Angus again with satisfaction.

"But we couldn't agree," said Kirstie.

"Got any ideas?" said Grumble to Mother.

Mother thought for a minute. "Well, he was washed up on the shore, wasn't he?" she said. "He was a castaway. And the most famous storybook castaway I can think of was Robinson Crusoe. How about that?"

"Now there's an idea!" said Grumble to the children. "That story was based on a real-life castaway, and he was called Alexander Selkirk and he was a Scot! And whatever the Water Horse is, there's no doubt about one thing. He's a Scottish beastie!"

"Robinson Crusoe," said Kirstie doubt-fully. "It's rather long, isn't it?"

"Just Crusoe then," said Angus. Grumble and Kirstie looked at one another and nodded.

"A good decision," they said.

But the decision they had to make after breakfast was not so easy. It was, of course, what to do with the newly christened Crusoe. They stood looking down at him as he paddled around the tub, chirruping loudly for food.

"Now, I've been thinking," Grumble said. "First of all, d'you think we should simply put him back in the sea? That's where he would have hatched if the storm hadn't blown him ashore."

"Oh, no!" said Kirstie. "We'd never see him again. Couldn't we find a big rock pool and keep him there?"

"We could. But the spring tides might wash him out. Anyway, it'd be a terrible business feeding him, up and down the cliff path half a dozen times a day."

"Could we put him in the lochan, Grumble?" said Angus. The lochan was a small loch, no bigger than a couple of soccer fields, in the glen below the house.

"We could, Angus, and that's where he'll have to go when he's a lot bigger. But he wouldn't last long at the moment. There are pike in there big enough to swallow him whole," said Grumble, and he picked up a sardine by its tail and dropped it into the bathtub. With a swirl of water, Crusoe was on it, worrying it like a shark.

"We must wait till he's big enough to treat the pike like that," said Grumble.

"But where *can* we keep him?" said Kirstie.

"I know!" said Grumble. "In the goldfish pond, of course. I don't know why I didn't think of it straightaway."

Sunk in the lawn at one side of the white house was an oblong concrete pond the size of a pool table. In it lived two goldfish named Janet and John that Kirstie had won at a fair when she was no older than Angus. Since then she had in fact taken no notice at all of them, but the sight now of Crusoe tearing chunks out of a sardine made her blood run cold.

"Oh, no!" she cried. "What about Janet and John?"

"Lunch and dinner," said Angus dryly.

"No, no," said Grumble. "We can't have that. We'll mount a rescue operation. We'll fish 'em out with the shrimping net. There's an old goldfish bowl in my garden shed. They can live in that till Crusoe's big enough to move to the lochan. Now, one of you can come and help me catch them, and one of you can feed this fellow the rest of the can."

Kirstie looked at her little brother. His eyes were glued to the remaining sardines. "I'll stay here," she said quickly.

When the others had gone, she knelt by the side of the bathtub, balancing the sardine can on the rim, and began to feed the Water Horse. She fed him very small scraps of fish.

"Gulping your food is bad for you," she said. "Grumble shouldn't have given you a whole one like that." Crusoe looked directly at her. His eyes, she noticed, were lozenge-shaped, very dark, and bright with a look of intelligence. He seemed to be listening to what she was saying.

When he had finished the third of the four sardines, he appeared to be full, for he sank to the bottom of the bathtub and lay there for a little while. Then he floated up like a bubble rising in a fizzy drink, poked his nostrils out, drew a breath of air, and sank again. He continued to do this, and Kirstie timed him with her watch.

She found he was able to hold his breath for about a minute, and his rises for air seemed quite automatic since his eyes were shut and he seemed to be fast asleep. After around a quarter of an hour of this, Crusoe surfaced properly and looked up at Kirstie once more. He did not, however, chirrup.

"You've had enough, haven't you?" said Kirstie. "We'll keep the last sardine for later." Her fingers were oily, and she was just about to rinse them in the water when it occurred to her that Crusoe just might treat them as he had treated the fish.

"Don't be such a baby, Kirstie," she said to herself. "His teeth aren't all that big, and anyway it will never do to let him think I'm afraid of him." So she put one finger down slowly, saying all the while in a quiet voice, "Good boy, Crusoe, good boy," until it was touching his nose.

Very gently, he licked it.

4

The Last Sardine

IT NEVER ENTERED Crusoe's head to bite
the finger that was extended to him. The
giant creature to whom it belonged was
simply, in his mind, a provider of food and
thus a good friend to him, as were they all.

This one now began to tickle him as he
lay floating, flippers spread, on the surface.
Gently the tickling fingers moved down
from his horse head and along the toad skin
of his turtle back to his crocodile tail.
The sensation was delicious, and Crusoe
squirmed in pleasure, eyes shut in ecstasy.
When he opened them again, it was to see
that two more of the giants had returned,
and once more they all began to make

strange sounds at one another. Now the smallest giant took over the tickling, rather more roughly, which somehow increased Crusoe's delight. He wriggled so much that little wavelets spread and slapped against the sides of the bathtub.

That's the only complaint I have, said Crusoe to himself. The food's yummy, the tickling's great, and the giants are obviously very decent creatures. But I am beginning to feel cramped in this small cold white prison. I wish they had somewhere bigger to put me. At that precise moment the biggest giant—as though he were a mind reader—bent over and picked Crusoe out of the bathtub.

Most of us can remember a few particular things from our early childhood, and all his immensely long life the Water Horse never forgot the moment when he was launched into the goldfish pond.

He did not know what it was, of course, only that it was ten times the size of the place he had come from, and deep, and

dark, and weedy. Excitedly he paddled all
around it, and then dived beneath its carpet
of water lilies and began to scrabble around
in the mud in which they were rooted. This

action disturbed a host of tiny pond dwellers, freshwater shrimp and diving beetles and wiggly wormy things, and off went Crusoe in hot pursuit. Now, with room to move, he was already showing quite a turn of speed, and he caught and swallowed several of them; but most were too quick for him, and at last he surfaced, breathless, to see that the fourth giant had joined the other three to watch him.

The Water Horse chirruped loudly at them. It was in fact the only noise he was capable of making so far, and he did it now simply because he felt happy. But its effect was immediate, for instantly the last of the sardines landed before his nose with an oily splash.

"That's the last he gets of my sardines," said Mother. "Do you understand that, all of you?"

"The last one ever?" said Kirstie. "Couldn't he have one for a treat, now and again?"

"At Christmas," said Angus, "and Easter and on his birthday and on Saturdays and Sundays and..."

"No," said Mother. "He couldn't. It's hard enough to make ends meet feeding the three of you, without wasting good food on a...whatever you said it was."

"Water Horse," they chorused.

"It's not a waste, Mother," said Angus. "He needs it if he's going to grow into a really big monster."

Grumble pulled at his droopy mustache and glowered at Mother from under his bushy eyebrows in quite his old grumpy manner. "Would you begrudge the poor beastie a square meal?" he growled.

"Yes," said Mother. "If you want to spend your pension buying food for it, that's your business. I daresay it would prefer smoked salmon?" And she marched off into the house.

Kirstie looked at Crusoe going after the last sardine with gusto.

"I could save some of my food and give

it to him," she said. "You could too, Angus, couldn't you?"

"No," said Angus.

"There's no need for this talk of saving food, much less of buying it," said Grumble. "What we have to do is catch it for Crusoe."

"Fish, you mean?" said Kirstie.

"Fish, yes, and anything else we can find for him, in the sea, on the beach, in the rock pools. I doubt he'll be fussy, so long as it's something with flesh on it." He looked at Crusoe, in the act of swallowing the sardine's tail.

"He's a carnivore, all right," he said.

"What's that?" said Angus.

"A meat eater," said Kirstie.

"I'm a carnivore," said Angus.

"You're an omnivore," said Grumble.

"What's that?" said Angus.

"Somebody who eats anything and everything," said Grumble.

Crusoe, having finished the fish, paddled to the edge of the goldfish pond, laid his horse head on the concrete rim, and chirruped.

"He's still hungry," said Kirstie, though in fact he was asking for a nice tickle.

"So am I," said Angus. "It must be time for tea." And he trudged off.

"D'you know, Grumble," said Kirstie, "Crusoe looks bigger to me already, although he isn't even one day old yet."

Grumble knelt down and, stretching out a hand, put his thumb on Crusoe's nose and opened his fingers as wide as they would go. The little finger touched the tip of the Water Horse's tail. "He's exactly my span," he said.

"How long is that?"

"Nine inches."

"How long d'you think he'll be when he's full-grown?"

"Fifty or sixty feet."

"Oh, Grumble, you're pulling my leg! He'd have to grow fantastically quickly."

"He will," said Grumble. "You mark my words."

And, only twenty-four hours later, Kirstie marked them.

They had had a successful morning's expedition down to the beach, Kirstie and Angus hunting through the rock pools with a shrimping net each, and Grumble, wearing a pair of tall waders, trawling through the shallows with the big prawning net. The children had found a number of little rockfish, blennies, and gobies, and Grumble had caught a couple of fair-sized dabs.

Crusoe had had the dabs for lunch, and now, at teatime, was just polishing off the last of the rockfish. When he had finished, he came to the pool's edge as before. Angus had already gone into the house. "It makes me hungry just watching him," he had said.

Grumble knelt down and made a span of his hand. Stretch it as he might, the little finger could not reach the tail tip.

"He's grown an inch!" cried Kirstie. "A whole inch! In a day!"

And as the days passed, the Water Horse grew and grew.

Feeding him was less of a problem than one might have thought, for as Grumble had forecast, he was not the least bit choosy. In addition to various kinds of fish, he happily tucked into prawns and shrimps and starfish and easily crunched up quite large green shore crabs. He particularly liked mussels, fortunately, for the rocks were thick with them, and the children spent a lot of time opening them for him.

The fact that all these were saltwater creatures, released into the fresh water of the goldfish pond, presented no problems. They did not last long enough to be troubled by the change, for Crusoe's appetite was growing as fast as his body. And his body, as the weeks passed, had already grown from kitten size to cat size. At one month of age, when Grumble measured him, he needed two spans, thumb to thumb, to reach from nose to tail.

"When d'you think he'll be big enough to go in the lochan, Grumble?" Kirstie asked.

"Not yet," said Grumble. "There's pike in there twice that size."

"But he'd beat 'em up, I bet he'd beat 'em up!" shouted Angus. "He'd bite chunks out of those old pike, Crusoe would! He'd tear 'em to bits!" and he ran around and around the pond, paddling his arms like flippers and roaring and making horrible biting faces.

"No, no," said Grumble, "he needs to be a lot bigger yet. We must keep on cramming him full of food for a good while longer, till he can look after himself and protect himself. After all, the great thing is that, here in the goldfish pond, Crusoe is perfectly safe."

But Grumble was wrong.

5

In the Midst of Foes

THERE'S A LINE in a very old hymn that says "Thou art in the midst of foes," and, though none of them realized it, Crusoe was.

The first foe came on four feet.

Early one morning when Crusoe was three months old, Kirstie awoke just before dawn to hear a noise in the distance. It was a sharp fluty whistle. Mother heard it too, took it for a bird, turned over, and went to sleep again. Grumble, wakeful in the early part of the night as old people often are, had dropped off at last. Angus, of course, was in the deepest of sleeps and heard nothing.

The whistle came again.

Behind the small white house on the cliff top was moorland, great stretches of heather and peat bog where curlew trilled their sad bubbling cries and the red grouse shouted, "Go back! Go back!" But whatever was whistling was coming closer, coming off the moor toward the house.

And suddenly an awful thought struck Kirstie, so that she jumped out of bed and grabbed a book from her bookcase. It was called *Wild Animals of the British Isles*, and was, because she was interested in such things, a favorite of hers. Something she had been reading in it quite recently rang alarm bells in her mind, and hastily she found the page she wanted. She skimmed hurriedly through "Life History," "Yearly Life," "Daily Life," and "Food," until she came to "Voice." "A hiss when playful or scared," it read. "A squeal when angry. A sharp fluty whistle..."

Even as she read it, the noise came again, very near now—the whistle of an otter!

Throwing on her bathrobe, Kirstie

rushed downstairs, stamped her bare feet into her boots, and dashed out of the house. It was light enough now to see—to see as she ran—a long low-slung hump-backed shape crossing the grass toward the goldfish pond. Otters, Kirstie knew, ate all sorts of fish, and to this one the Water Horse would be just another, different, kind.

She opened her mouth and let out the loudest yell she'd ever yelled in her life, and a very surprised and startled otter turned and galloped away as fast as its short legs would carry it.

Kirstie knelt by the pond, panting from the effort of running and from the mixture of fear and anger that had gripped her, and in a moment the sleeping form of Crusoe floated up. His nose poked out and he took a breath and sank again. He had heard nothing of Kirstie's shout. Nor, of course, had Angus, but soon Mother and Grumble came hurrying to see what was the matter.

"What can we do?" asked Kirstie when

she had told them. "The otter might come again."

"I doubt it will," said Grumble. "The noise you made was enough to frighten the life out of it. It certainly frightened me. But, just in case, we must take steps to protect Crusoe."

And that morning Grumble made a big frame, a wooden frame with wire netting stretched over it, which fitted over the top of the pond like a lid. Throughout the rest of that summer it remained there, day and night, only lifted off when Crusoe was being fed or played with.

The second foe came on two feet.

It was a month or so later, in the autumn now, and it just so happened that no one was at home. Mother had caught the bus to do the week's shopping, and the others had gone down to the sea, to beachcomb and to catch food for Crusoe. He would be safe, they thought, under his wire lid.

They had nearly reached the top of the cliff path on their way back, Grumble carrying a load of driftwood and the children a bucket of fish each, when suddenly they heard, from the direction of the goldfish pond, a sudden loud harsh croaking noise. "Frank!" was what it sounded like, and it was repeated, hurriedly, frantically it seemed: "Frank! Frank! Frank!"

"Quick!" shouted Grumble, throwing down his load. "Put down those buckets and run!"

"What is it?" cried the children.

"A heron!"

Oh, no! thought Kirstie as she ran. Not only had she read about them in her book, but she had seen a heron before now, standing in the shallows of the lochan on its long legs, long neck outstretched, peering forward into the water. She had seen it pause, motionless, and then with lightning speed stab downward with its long yellow beak and spear a fish.

But the scene that met their eyes was more comic than tragic.

The heron had indeed tried to stab the Water Horse, but the point of its beak was

now stuck in the wire mesh of the protective frame. "Frank!" cried the bird again, tugging madly to free itself at the sight of the approaching humans. And at last it succeeded, and, jumping into the air, flew away with slow flaps of its great curved wings.

"There's blood in the water," said Angus somberly, and indeed the tip of the heron's bill had gone far enough through the wire to nick Crusoe's back. But it was not much more than a scratch and he did not seem too worried about it. At any rate, he ate all the fish that they had caught with his usual gusto.

The third foe came in the winter, not on four legs or two. It had no substance, could not be seen or smelled or heard. But whereas the coming of the first two foes was a surprise, the arrival of the third was actually broadcast.

One evening early in the new year, Grumble sat listening, as was his custom, to the radio, waiting for the weather forecast so that he could, as was his custom, grumble about it.

And then news of the third foe came out of the radio.

"Tonight," said a voice, "there will be widespread frost in Scotland. It will be severe in the Highland and Grampian areas, though only slight in the western parts."

As usual, the west coast of Scotland was to come off lightly, thanks to the warm waters of the Gulf Stream flowing to it across the Atlantic. But the threat of even a slight frost was enough to put Grumble on his guard. On checking it last thing that night, he found the surface of the goldfish pond still unfrozen, protected perhaps by the wire screen. But by first thing next morning there was a thin skin of ice on the pond.

Before breakfast he stood with the children and watched as Crusoe, obviously enjoying himself, rammed his way through the ice, breaking it up with a crackling noise.

"He's an icebreaker!" shouted Angus, running around the pond, arms outstretched and fingertips together in the shape of a ship's prow. "An icebreaker in the Antarctic, old Crusoe is, full speed ahead, crash, bang, wallop!"

"But before too long he may not be able to break it," said Grumble to Kirstie.

"Why not?"

"Because they're saying now that this is the start of a really cold spell, and in a few days' time a small pond like this could be frozen very thick."

"Too thick for Crusoe to break?" said Kirstie.

"Could be."

"Thick enough to slide on?" said Angus, coming to a halt. "That would be fun!"

"It wouldn't be any fun for Crusoe, you silly boy," said Kirstie. "If he was stuck under the ice, he couldn't breathe."

"He'd drown," said Angus in a solemn voice. He clasped both hands around his throat, stuck out his tongue, crossed his eyes, and made dreadful gurgling noises of suffocation.

"Oh, don't be so stupid," Kirstie said. "Grumble, what can we do?"

"We'll have to move him."

"To the lochan?"

"Yes, that will never freeze."

"But the pike? The otter? The heron?"

"I reckon he's big enough to look after himself now."

And indeed, the Water Horse, now ten months old, had grown enormously. The pond had long been empty of animal life except for him, since he had eaten every-thing in it, and his demands for food meant that for some time now it had been neces-sary to make two trips a day to the beach. He was as big as...well, it's difficult to measure such an animal against a different one, but since the comparison was first with a kitten, then a cat, you could say that now, though he looked nothing like one, he was the size and weight of a half-grown tiger. Like a tiger's, his body had grown very long, though of course he did not have legs and feet, but simply those four big diamond-shaped flippers.

"Big enough to look after himself!" said Angus. "Blow me down, I should think he is! I bet he could beat up that old otter and that old heron now, Grumble! He'd shiver their timbers all right!"

"But how are we going to move him?" asked Kirstie.

"That's what's worrying me," said Grumble. "I've waited a bit too long. I had planned to get him into the wheelbarrow

A view of the loch.

Old Angus MacMorrow tells some visitors about Crusoe, the Water Horse.

Young Angus MacMorrow finds a strange object in a tide pool.

Angus brings the object home and carefully examines it on the counter of his father's workroom.

After scraping off the outer layers of shells and seaweed, Angus finds that the object has a shiny, almost metallic surface.

Angus returns to the workroom to find that the object is on the floor, broken in two, and is empty inside. It appears to be a *hatched egg!*

In a flashback, young Angus listens to his dad talk about the Water Horse.

Angus and his sister, Kirstie, run through the house, looking for young Crusoe, who has escaped.

Churchill, a bulldog, chases Crusoe near the water fountain.

Lewis Mobray watches as Crusoe swims out into the loch for the first time.

Townsman Jimmy McGarry sees Crusoe for the first time while fishing on Loch Ness.

Angus rows out onto the loch, looking for his friend Crusoe.

Angus tells Mobray and Kirstie about his adventure with Crusoe earlier that day.

Sunset on the loch.

Kirstie and Ann MacMorrow, Angus's mother, listen to Angus as he talks about Crusoe.

Jimmy McGarry and Jock McGowan, a folklorist and a reporter for the local newspaper, take a photograph of "the Monster"—a fake one that they've built.

Churchill smells Crusoe and tries to track him down.

Angus calls
out to Crusoe
as Mobray
looks on.

Angus, Ann, Lewis, Kirstie, and Captain Hamilton run to
see Crusoe.

Angus points up at
Crusoe.

Ann sees Crusoe for the first time.

Angus and Ann look out over the loch.

Angus and Kirstie watch as Crusoe heads out to sea.

somehow, but I doubt I could do that on my own, and I can't ask anyone else or the secret of the Water Horse would be out and that would never do. This is the problem. I really need the help of a strong man."

"What shall we do?" said Kirstie.

"Let's have breakfast," said Angus. "I'm starving."

As they walked toward the house, they caught sight of Postie, the mailman, riding away down the road on his old red bicycle, and when they came into the kitchen, Mother was standing there with an opened letter in her hand. She looked very happy.

"Guess what!" she said to the children. "It's from your father! His ship berthed in the Clyde yesterday. He'll be home this very morning!"

6

Home Is the Sailor

KIRSTIE WAS SO excited at the thought of Father coming home on leave that she could not manage to eat much. Angus was excited too, but that didn't keep him from finishing his own breakfast and Kirstie's leftovers.

Because they knew what time the bus arrived at the stop at the bottom of the glen, they were ready and waiting on the road outside the small white house when the distant blue-clad figure appeared, duffel bag on shoulder, packages under one arm, waving happily with the other.

"Home is the sailor, home from sea," said Grumble contentedly to himself as he watched Mother and the children running to greet him.

At first it was all excitement in the house as the packages were opened, presents from far, distant lands. For Mother there was a length of beautiful silk, for Grumble a packet of strange foreign seeds to plant in the garden, for Kirstie a necklace made of sharks' teeth, and for Angus a four-masted ship with a full spread of canvas, sailing eternally within its bottle.

"How you've grown!" said Father to the children. "Why, last leave I was carrying you about easily, Angus. I wouldn't be able to now."

"He likes his food," said Mother.

All this reminded Kirstie of the Water Horse and how he had grown too heavy to carry.

"Grumble!" she cried. "We haven't fed Crusoe yet!"

"Who's Crusoe?" said Father.

"He's our monster!" shouted Angus. "We found him on the beach and he hatched in the bathtub, and he lives in the goldfish pond, and we catch fish for him every day, and he gobbles them up, chomp, chomp, chomp. You should see his teeth, Father, miles bigger than the ones on Kirstie's necklace, they are!" and Angus made frightening chewing faces.

"Whatever's the boy talking about?" said Father, and the others explained everything to him.

"You couldn't have come home at a better time," said Grumble. "We must get him into the lochan, the quicker the better, and he's too heavy for me to manage. Getting him out of the goldfish pond won't be easy, to begin with, so my idea is not to feed him at all today, and then he'll be so hungry that he might manage to climb out himself if we tempt him with something tasty."

"Come and see him, Father," said Kirstie, and they all went out to the pond where Crusoe was calling hungrily.

They took off the wire frame, and Kirstie said "Crusoe!" and the Water Horse came and laid his head on the rim of the pond.

"Holy mackerel!" said Father. "I've sailed the seven seas and never seen such a creature! Is it some kind of sea serpent?"

"A Water Horse," said Grumble.

"I've heard you speak of such a thing. Was there not one in Loch Morar, I think you told me once?"

Grumble nodded. "Gentle him," he said. "He's an amiable beastie."

And Father bent down and scratched and pulled at Crusoe's ears. "When shall we try to move him, then?" he said.

"In the morning, I thought," said Grumble. "Between us we can maybe get him into my old wheelbarrow and wheel him down the road to the lochan. It's a Sunday, so Postie will not be coming and there's no bus and not likely to be anyone else about."

Crusoe had been swimming rapidly up and down the length of the goldfish pond, as he always did as midday approached, raising his horse head at intervals to gaze in the direction of the top of the cliff path. It was at this time that he received his first meal of the day. Now, when he saw the giants approaching, he began to call out impatiently. He could no longer be said to chirrup, for his voice had broken, so that he made a kind of rough bellow, like a cow

with a sore throat calling for its calf. It was a hoarse noise, you might say.

But when the giants arrived and removed the wire frame, he could see that they had brought no food. Moreover, there were now not four of them, but five. One of the smaller ones called his name, and at the sound he came, as he was now accustomed, and laid his head upon the rim of the pond. The new giant—another very large one, with a good deal of hair on its chin—bent down and scratched and pulled pleasantly at his ears, and they all made their usual medley of sounds, some deep, some shrill.

Then they went away, and as they disappeared, a steady cold rain began to fall. By evening the rain had stopped, but by then Crusoe was very hungry. He had had nothing at all to eat for twenty-four hours now, and his mind was filled with tantalizing visions of food—tender spotted dabs and fat little brown rockfish, and crunchy green crabs and juicy pink starfish. As for mussels, he could have eaten a barrel of them.

For the first time in his life he felt the need to go looking for food instead of waiting for it to be brought to him, and for the first time he actually tried to get out of the goldfish pond. After a great deal of clumsy effort, he managed to lift the wire frame with his head and get both front flippers up onto the rain-soaked concrete rim, but it was too steep and already frozen, and he slipped back with a moan of disappointment.

That night the frost was much more severe. But the surface of the pond had no chance to freeze over, because Crusoe's hunger pangs kept him swimming around urgently.

Dawn came, and the sun rose and climbed in the sky and shone down without warmth, and the ravenous Water Horse bellowed his hunger to the frozen world. And then at long last, four of the giants appeared again, and as they came closer, he could smell the food that they were carrying!

Father and the others could see that though there had been a hard frost, Crusoe had kept the pond ice-free, paddling hungrily about. But everything else was ice-covered, for the previous afternoon's rain had frozen solid upon every surface. Even the branches and twigs of the trees were coated in ice.

Crusoe came eagerly to the side without waiting to be called. He could smell the fish that Kirstie was carrying on a plate.

To everyone's surprise (and to Angus's dismay), Mother had donated a small can of herring as bait to lure the Water Horse out of the pond. Actually, she was delighted to think that he was going somewhere where he could catch his own food from now on, freeing her from the endless washing of clothes covered in slimy fish scales.

"Hold one of the herring in front of his nose, Kirstie," said Grumble. "Not too near, mind. Don't let him get it yet."

Frantically Crusoe tried to haul himself out, but the icy rim was too slippery.

"Right," said Father. "We'll have to help him." The moving of heavy weights in and out of ships' holds was something he well understood, and now he took charge.

"Angus," he said, "take station abaft me. I reckon this fellow weighs closer to two hundred pounds than a hundred, and we don't want anyone getting hurt. Kirstie, keep the fish right in front of his face but be ready to go full astern as he comes out." And to Grumble he said, "Next time he comes up on the rim, I'll take ahold of one front flipper and you take the other and wait for my word. Ready? Now, Kirstie!" And as Crusoe reared up once again, Father and Grumble each grabbed a flipper.

"Heave!" shouted Father, and "Heave!" while Angus danced around, yelling, "Come on, my hearties!" And at last, with much grunting and sloshing, the Water Horse came out of the goldfish pond and lay dripping on the frozen grass.

"Belay!" said Father to Grumble, and to Kirstie, "Give him the fish."

"Phew!" said Grumble. "He *is* heavy! I doubt we'll get him into the wheelbarrow."

"If we did," said Father, "and it didn't break under him, I doubt we could push him. Let's see first if he'll sail under his own steam."

And so began a slow procession, from the pond, across the lawn, toward the road. Crusoe's grace and speed on or under water was equaled only by his clumsiness and sluggishness on land. But driven on by his hunger, he followed Kirstie and her herring, slowly, oh, so slowly, inching along at tortoise speed.

"What a rate of knots!" said Father, looking at his watch. "Half an hour to travel fifty yards!"

"We'll be here all day and night getting him to the lochan," growled Grumble. But then something happened that changed the whole picture.

Kirstie, walking backward still, reached the road at last and stepped off the shoulder onto the tarmac surface. Immediately, her legs shot from under her, and, as she fell, the last few herring flew off the plate and landed right in front of the grateful Water Horse.

"Are you all right, Kirstie?" everyone shouted.

"Yes," she said, struggling to her feet, "but he's eaten all the fish now. What else can we tempt him with?"

"We shan't need to," said Father, grinning.

"Why not?"

"Look," said Father, and he found a smooth pebble and skimmed it down the slight slope of the road. On and on it slid, for the rain on the surface of the road had frozen into a thick slippery surface like a skating rink.

"We can slide him!" said Grumble. "Like a curling stone!"

And that's exactly what they did.

The road was so glassy that Father made Grumble and the children walk on the shoulder, for young bones and old bones are easily broken in a fall, he knew, and he took

upon himself the job of pushing Crusoe.

Now their progress was ten times as fast. Slipping, sliding, slithering, and skidding, the Water Horse glided down the icy road with no effort on his own part and very little on Father's, and in another half hour or so they had reached the lochan, a quarter of a mile away. Then it was easy. The edge of the lochan was close to the road and a little below it, and with one last concerted shove they launched Crusoe into his new home.

It was easy to see his delight at being back in his element again, and at finding so much space to swim in. Away he went, head and neck showing above the surface like a periscope, a V-shaped wake streaming out behind him, until he reached the middle of the lochan. There he turned, and for a moment looked back at them standing on the shore.

Then he slid silently beneath the surface and was lost to their sight.

7

A Bit Too Tame

"YOU SEE THE problem, don't you?" said Father on the following morning.

"I do," said Grumble. "He's a bit too tame."

They watched the children standing in the shallows, playing with Crusoe. Each had a stick to scratch his back, and as usual he was squirming with pleasure at the rough tickling.

There had been no sign of him when they arrived. The surface of the lochan was calm and empty, but Kirstie had called "Crusoe!" and almost at once he had surfaced and come swimming toward them.

"He's not afraid of humans, that's the

73

trouble," said Father. "Kind treatment and good food—that's what people mean to him. So now he'll react the same way to anybody, I'm thinking—one of the locals, a tourist, anyone." He turned to the children. "Suppose a couple of your school friends were coming to visit you, and Crusoe spotted them—he might come for a tickle, mistaking them for you. You've not told any of the children at school, have you?"

"Of *course* not!" said Kirstie, shocked.

"They wouldn't believe me if I did," said Angus.

"Anyway," said Grumble, "there's not many folk come this way."

"But it only needs one person to see him," said Father, "and that will give the game away. Then we'll have dozens of newspaper reporters writing about him, taking photographs of him, and then the world and his wife will want to come and gawk at him. Next thing, they'll want to catch him and put him in a zoo. That's if some sportsman doesn't shoot him first and mount his head and stick it on the wall for a trophy."

"The lochan's so small," said Grumble, "specially at the rate he's growing. Now, if only we could put him in a really huge stretch of water—Loch Lomond, say—he'd not be so easy to spot."

"Hmm," said Father. "In my opinion," he said, "the first thing to be done is to teach him a new trick. He comes when he's called. Now we must train him to stay hidden *unless* he's called."

"How on earth are we to do that?"

"It won't be easy. It means disciplining the animal. He's had things too easy—that's the trouble."

"The children are awful fond of the beastie," said Grumble. "They get a lot of pleasure from him."

"You've a soft spot for him yourself, I'm thinking," said Father. He shot a glance at his father-in-law's face, which wore an unaccustomed smile as he watched his grandchildren at play with the Water Horse. "If you don't mind my saying so," he went on, "you're a happier man than you used to be."

"Hmm!" growled Grumble.

"Anyway," said Father, "if we're to keep this strange pet—and that means keeping him a secret—then he's going to have to learn the hard way that he must show himself only when we want him to, when we summon him."

That evening as they all sat around a good fire of driftwood, for it was still very cold outside, Father explained things to the children.

"So you see," he finished, "this is what we must do, unless we want to risk losing Crusoe. If we call him by name and he comes, that's fine—we can pat him and praise him and tickle him and offer him tidbits and make a thorough fuss of him. But what we must also do, many times during the next few weeks"—Father had a month's leave while his ship was refitting at Greenock—"is to go and stand by the lochan and *not* call him, not say anything.

He'll see us and come anyway at first, but when he does, we don't touch him, don't give him anything, only speak sharply, angrily to him as you would to a dog that had done something naughty."

"Oh, but Father!" said Kirstie. "Crusoe's feelings will be terribly hurt!"

"Maybe they will. But he'll learn. He *must* learn, we must teach him, and we can't start too soon. First lesson tomorrow morning."

The previous day had been a memorable one for Crusoe—his emergence from the goldfish pond, his painful progress toward the road, the strange dizzy sensation of sliding giddily down the hill, and finally the glorious feeling of finding himself free in a watery home hundreds of times bigger than the old one. He had swum out through the still dark waters effortlessly, turned to see the four giants watching him and waving at him, and dived down, down into the depths. And what was in those depths? Fish, fish, thousands and thousands of them! Crusoe didn't know a pike from a perch or a salmon from a trout. All he knew was that the lochan was alive with food—food that was now, he found, easy for him to catch, so swiftly could he move underwater.

By nightfall he had gorged himself and tired himself out in the bargain, and with the simplicity that marked all his actions, he closed his eyes and went to sleep. As always, he rose automatically in the midst of his slumbers to refill his lungs with air, and as automatically sank down again, not six feet now but sixty.

The next morning after he had breakfasted, he was swimming idly along in what was, had he known it, the natural and instinctive manner of his race when not hunting. That is to say, he was completely submerged and thus invisible to an onlooker—except for his two nostrils, which were just above the surface of the water.

Then he heard the call that was, had he known it, his name, and he swam rapidly to shore.

What a joy it was to be tickled by the two smallest giants (he still thought of them that way, though he was now far bigger than either of them), and how he wriggled with pleasure! That they did not feed him mattered not at all for he was full. Full and extremely happy.

But on the following day things were very different!

He must have been underwater when the giants arrived, for he did not know they were there until he suddenly caught sight of the four of them, standing silently on the shore. No call came from them, but Crusoe, delighted to see them, swam straight toward them and sploshed his way up into the shallows, where he lay, staring up at them lovingly, waiting for a tickle. But no tickle was forthcoming, nor any of the usual affectionate sounds. Instead, they made what sounded like angry noises, and pointed out to the middle of the lochan, and shooed him away as if they wanted nothing more to do with him. And then they turned and left without a backward look.

Puzzled and hurt, the Water Horse stared after the departing giants. What had he done wrong? He bowed his head and gave a low moan of distress.

8

First Birthday

"IT WAS AWFUL!" said Kirstie to Mother. "Turning away and just leaving him. How can he know he's done anything wrong?" Her eyes filled with tears.

Mother gave her a cuddle. "I'm sure he'll soon learn," she said.

"It's bound to be hard for him at first," said Father, "but it's the only thing to do."

"He'll be happy enough with all those fish to eat," said Grumble. "Why, his stomach looked as tight as a drum."

"When's lunch?" said Angus.

They went down again that afternoon. Kirstie called Crusoe and he came and they all made a tremendous fuss over him, so that she was much happier when she went to bed that night.

But as soon as she awoke the next morning, she felt miserable to think that she must once again pretend to be angry with him if he came without being called. And of course he did, and the whole performance of berating and shooing him was repeated.

For several days there was no sign that he understood, but then one morning they went down to the lochan and stood, silent, and the Water Horse did *not* come. They could see his head clear of the water over on the far side, watching them, but he did not move.

"Better," said Father, "but not good enough. Anyone could see that great noodle sticking up." And he shouted "DIVE! DIVE! DIVE!" in a loud sailor's bellow. The head submerged with a startled splash.

Gradually, it seemed as though the Water Horse was getting the message. Before long, he never came unless called, and by the time Father went back to rejoin his ship, the others were all confident that, unless they shouted his name, they could not see a hair on his head (if he'd had any hair). Somewhere a pair of nostrils would be protruding just above the water, perhaps even a pair of watching eyes, but no one could ever have spotted them amongst the shifting ripples of the surface.

Now at last there was no longer any need to speak harshly to Crusoe. The lesson had been learned, and they could simply enjoy spoiling him each time he answered his name, and he could enjoy the tickling and the warm words of praise and, now, the occasional treat of a special (and, for the Water Horse, unusual) tidbit.

One day Angus had arrived carrying a cookie in his hand. It was his habit to provide himself with emergency supplies of some sort, to see him through the difficult gap between one meal and the next. But on this occasion—maybe because it was not long after breakfast—he had reached the lochan without having yet eaten the cookie. It was chocolate chip, his favorite kind.

They called Crusoe and stood waiting on the bank, when, so suddenly as to make them jump, he surfaced right beside them, stretched out his long neck, and took the chocolate chip cookie neatly out of Angus's hand.

"Avast, there!" shouted Angus angrily. "Give that back, you son of a sea cook!" But the cookie had vanished and a pleased expression had appeared upon the face of the Water Horse. He licked his lips in appreciation and gave a short deep grunt, a sign, they knew, of great contentment.

From then on, by common consent (with the exception of Angus), a chocolate chip cookie was Crusoe's special treat, and on March the 27th, 1931, they gave him a whole box as a first birthday present.

"Do you remember, Grumble," said Kirstie as they watched the box disappear, cardboard and all, "when he was only as long as the span of your hand? Just look at him now!"

Now, it was of no use trying to describe Crusoe's size as matching that of any kind of tiger, even a sabertooth. He was far bigger. Grumble reckoned that at the end of that first year of life he measured roughly fifteen feet from nose to tail tip. "It's all the fish he's eating," he said.

"What happens," said Kirstie, "when he's caught all the fish in the lochan?" But before Grumble could answer, they heard a sound that was quite uncommon in those parts in those days. It was the sound of a car, farther down the glen and coming toward them.

"Dive!" snapped Grumble, and Crusoe instantly obeyed.

When the car reached them, it stopped on the road above, and the driver got out to ask directions from the big old man with the droopy mustache who stood by the lochan hand in hand with a girl and a small tubby boy.

"Thanks awfully," said the driver when Grumble had given him directions. He looked at the mirror-still surface of the lochan. "I say, what a peaceful spot!" he said. "Nothing ever disturbs it, I should imagine."

They waited until the sound of the departing car had died away, and then Grumble said, "Call him, Angus," and Angus shouted,

"Crusoe! Ahoy there, Crusoe!" and up out of the center of the lochan in a great fountain of water like a breaching whale rose the weird and wonderful shape of the Water Horse. In a flurry of spray and foam he hurtled shoreward at his best speed, bellowing softly with pleasure at this second summons from his friends.

"I say, what a peaceful spot!" drawled Angus. "Nothing ever disturbs it, I should imagine."

Nothing did disturb it, throughout that spring and summer of 1931. Grumble took the children down to the lochan less frequently now, perhaps only once a week. When they asked why, he said that Crusoe needed to get more used to being on his own. It was like a child growing up, Grumble said: before long he would have to make his own way in the world.

But one day in the autumn they witnessed an incident that showed that Crusoe's tastes in food were not confined to fish (and chocolate chip cookies).

As they approached the usually deserted lochan, they saw, standing on the road above it, a party of about a dozen people. They were certainly not locals, for there was nothing Scottish in the loud voices that they could hear, and they were all oddly dressed. They wore pants—men and women alike—and thick Fair Isle sweaters and heavy hobnailed boots, and they had knapsacks on their backs and carried stout walking sticks.

"Who are they?" said Angus.

"Hikers," said Grumble sourly.

"What are hikers?" said Kirstie.

"Folk who tramp all over the countryside, townsfolk mostly. It's all the fashion these days. Don't know a sheep from a pig." Just then they saw one of the hikers point out across the lochan, and then the whole party turned and looked and pointed. Kirstie caught her breath. Had they seen Crusoe? She listened tensely to the loud voices.

"Look at that goose!" said one.

"That's not a goose," said another, one of those men who knows everything, "that's a swan."

"Look, it's put its head right under the water. Doesn't it look funny with its bottom sticking up in the air! Why's it doing that?"

"It's looking for fish," said the clever one.

"Now it's come up again."

"Now it's put its head down again."

And as Grumble and the children watched, the swan dived once more. Then, quite silently and suddenly, it disappeared beneath the surface.

"Where's it gone?" said the hikers.

"It's dived," said the clever one.

There was silence then for several minutes, until somebody said, "It's been underneath an awful long time."

"They can hold their breath," said the clever one, and the hikers turned away and tramped off down the road, swinging their walking sticks.

Out on the water, a few white feathers rose and floated on the surface.

9

Postie

CRUSOE SWALLOWED THE swan with ease and satisfaction. He was not fussy (as Grumble had guessed much earlier) and it made a good square meal and a welcome addition to his diet of fish and eels. He had lived in the lochan long enough now to have caused the fish supplies to shrink, and once he had realized that there was prey on top of the water as well as below it, a great many waterfowl, feeding or resting on the surface, went to satisfy his appetite.

The Water Horse took coot, moorhens, seagulls even, but especially duck. Those birds that fed by dabbling, like mallard and teal and wigeon, were sticking their necks out. As for the diving ducks, such as pochard and tufted duck, they were even easier meat for Crusoe, and he took several eider down to the bottom. Once, even a great northern diver went west.

All of which led him, one day, to bite off more than he could chew.

Another year had gone by. Father had been home on leave twice, marveling each time at Crusoe's growth. He was now nearly two and a half years old, and Father and Grumble were beginning to get worried. How much longer can he stay here? they asked each other. How long will the fish last? How long before he's so big that concealment in such a small loch is impossible?

One day in the late summer of 1932, something happened that made them worry even more.

It was the afternoon of a calm warm day, and Crusoe was taking his usual nap. It was his custom to have a good rest between the morning's and the evening's hunting, and as always, he slept underwater, rising for air at intervals. These, since he was so much bigger, could be as long as fifteen minutes. Now, as he floated very slowly up, nose tilted ready to draw an automatic breath, his snout bumped gently on something hard and he awoke. Sinking back down a little, he looked upward at the dark object that lay on the surface above his head. It was large, almost as large as himself, and was pointed at one end and squared off at the other. It was not moving.

What could that be? thought the Water Horse.

At that moment there was a little splash at some distance from the thing, and Crusoe swam over to investigate. But the length of line, with its hook and its silvery spinner, meant nothing to him, and he swam back beneath the dark object. He would have liked to stick his head out of the water and have a good look at it, but this, he knew, the giants would not like. They could not complain, surely, if he just took a little bite out of it?

Crusoe swam up, opened his jaws wide, and bit through the bottom of the boat.

Mother and the children had gone down to the beach and Grumble was alone in the small white house when he heard a knock at the door. He opened it, and there stood Postie, white-faced and dripping wet.

"Why, Mr. Macnab!" said Grumble. Postie, he knew, kept an old half-rotten dinghy tied up by the lochan and in his off-duty hours would sometimes try for the huge old pike that local folk believed to be lurking in its depths. "Did you tumble in, now?" he said.

"Tumble in!" said Postie. "Man, there's something awful big in the lochan! I felt a wee bump under the boat just before I cast, and then next minute there was a crunching noise and something tore the bottom

out of her. A hole the size of a frying pan
there was, and the water pouring in! She
sank before I could get her to shore, you
know. Boat, rod, and tackle—I've lost it all.
I was near drowned!"

You were near eaten, too, thought Grumble. He pulled thoughtfully at his mustache.

"What a pike that must be, Mr. Macnab," he said solemnly. "A monster, by the sound of it."

"That was no pike," said Postie. He cleared his throat. "Tell me now," he said hesitantly, "you live nearby...do you think there's anything living in the lochan?"

"Oh, aye!" said Grumble. "There's fish aplenty."

"I don't mean fish," said Postie. "I mean...have you ever seen..."—he dropped his voice to a whisper—"could it be...the kelpie?"

"Oh, Mr. Macnab," said Grumble, "you're surely not going to tell folk there's a kelpie in the lochan? I'm not saying that such creatures don't exist—there was one in Loch Morar when I was a boy—but for a man in your position to be saying such a thing, why, it would be most unwise."

"Unwise?" said Postie.

"Yes," said Grumble. "If it got about that someone like you—a responsible public servant entrusted with the delivery of His Majesty's Mail for miles around—was talking about seeing monsters, why, the powers that be in the Post Office might begin to doubt your fitness for the job. And there's a great deal of unemployment about these days, Mr. Macnab, so there is."

Postie stood and dripped for a moment. "So there is," he said. "Maybe you'll say nothing about this?"

"Not a word," said Grumble, and then, as if to seal the promise, "Now, you mustn't catch cold, so you'll take a wee dram with me before you go?"

"It could have been very nasty," he said later, when Mother and the children had heard the tale, "but I don't think Postie will say anything."

"Crusoe was good, though, wasn't he?" said Kirstie.

"Good?"

"Well, he didn't show himself."

"No, but he smashed up Postie's boat," said Mother.

"He shivered its timbers," said Angus.

10

A Harebrained Plan

CHRISTMAS 1932 WAS a good one in the small white house on the cliff top, because for once Father was at home for it. What's more, since his next voyage was to be a short one, he would have leave again, he told them, at the end of March or the beginning of April. "And by then the Water Horse will be three years old, isn't that right?" he said.

They nodded.

"And Heaven knows how much bigger he's going to grow," said Father. "We *must* move him. We must move him then, this coming spring, or else he'll likely be too big to move at all."

"But how can we, Father?" asked Kirstie.

"By road, of course."

"What in?"

"Well, what would you put a Water Horse in?"

"A horse trailer," said Angus.

"Not big enough."

"A moving van?" said Grumble.

"Difficult," said Father. "Moving vans are quite high off the ground and it would be very hard to load him. You'd need a crane, like we use at the docks. Anyway, what about the moving men? They'd be bound to see him and the story would be out. No, it seems to me there's only one kind of vehicle suitable for the job."

"A cattle truck!" said Mother.

"Exactly, you've got it. They're just big enough, they're strong enough to carry about a dozen bulls, they're covered so that he won't be seen on the journey, and they have a good long tail ramp to let down for him to scramble up. And one last thing—

there's a wee door at the front end of the body, just behind the cab, so that whoever goes into the truck before Crusoe to lure him in with food can get out without being squashed."

"Just one thing you've forgotten," said Grumble. "What about the driver of this cattle truck? There's no way of keeping things secret from him."

"There's no need," said Father. "He knows already. The driver of the cattle truck will be me." One of his shipmates, Father went on to explain, had a brother who was a cattle hauler in the district and would, he felt sure, rent out one of his trucks. "My pal tells me," said Father, "that his brother is not the most honest man in Scotland. Now and again, apparently, one of his trucks might pick up a bunch of cattle from an outlying field on a dark night and put them down in a different field forty or fifty miles away."

"Rustling, you mean?" said Grumble. Father nodded.

Mother looked worried. "You mean," she said, "that you're planning to let this hauler think you want his truck to go cattle rustling?"

Father grinned. "A nod and a wink and a bit of extra cash in his hand should do the trick," he said. "I've a clean driving license, and though I've never driven a truck, I expect I'll soon get the hang of it."

Mother opened her mouth to question such a crazy idea and then shut it again. Just as she had been pleased to see Crusoe's departure from the goldfish pond to the lochan, so now, she realized, she was glad to think he would be going many miles away, out of their lives forever, perhaps. It was not that she bore the Water Horse any ill will. It was simply that for nearly three years now he had occupied so much of everybody's time, besides demanding (she told herself, unfairly) constant supplies of sardines and herring and chocolate chip cookies. Her children, she felt (unfairly again), had neglected their homework and her father had done less in the garden. Now her husband was proposing to remove the creature. Good.

"Hmph!" she said, with the look and tone of Grumble. "I never heard of such a harebrained plan. I wash my hands of it," and she marched off to the kitchen to wash the dishes.

"But *where* are we going to take Crusoe?" asked Kirstie.

"It's got to be a really big loch, hasn't it?" asked Angus.

"You're right, Angus," said Father. "Get the map out of the drawer, will you? It's the one marked 'West Scotland: Islay to Gairloch.'" And when Angus had gotten it, Father spread it out on the table.

"Now, then," he said, "first of all, we could always put him in a sea loch. We could also let him go here, into Loch Moidart, and he'd be free to make his way anywhere in the world."

"No, no!" the children cried. "We'd never see him again!"

"Then it's one of three, isn't it?" said Grumble. "There's Loch Morar—that's the nearest sizable one to us, and deep, very deep. Maybe the Water Horse that was said to live in it when I was a boy is still there. Might be company for him."

"Wait, though," said Father, looking at the map. "See here—he could easily get down the River Morar to the sea. That's no good."

"Well, then, what about Loch Lomond? That's big enough."

"Too far," said Father. "I don't want to have to drive all that way."

"That only leaves one, then," said Grumble, and he pointed to a long blue stretch of water that ran diagonally up to the northeast. "Twenty-four miles from end to end and maybe the deepest of them all. There's all the space he could want there."

"You're right," said Father. "That's where we'll take Crusoe. That's the loch for him. And it's not as long a drive as all that—say, thirty miles to Fort William and another thirty to Fort Augustus."

"When he's living there," said Kirstie, "will we be able to visit him sometimes?" Her voice sounded a bit shaky.

"Of course we will," said Father. "It's no distance really, make a nice outing in the summer. We'll go and we'll call him and he'll come for a tickle."

"But suppose other people catch sight of him?"

"They could, I suppose," said Grumble, "now and again. If he's absent-minded and forgetful and shows himself for a moment. Or if he gets overexcited hunting fish near the surface. Or if he bumps a boat, like he did Postie's. We must just hope he behaves himself."

"Even if folk catch a glimpse of him, they're never going to be certain what they're seeing," said Father. "They'll think to themselves, oh, maybe it was just a log of wood or shadows on the water or salmon leaping or otters playing or a dead stag floating among the waves. They'll never be sure. We are the only people who will ever know for certain that in that loch there lives the Water Horse."

11

A Ride in a Truck

WHEN THE TIME came, loading Crusoe was easy.

There was a rough track that led down to the lochan from the road, and Father had reversed the cattle truck along it, stopping just short of the water where the ground grew soggy. Of Crusoe there was naturally no sign, since he had not been called.

Now, that spring morning, on April the 14th, 1933, everything was ready. The children sat safely inside the cab of the truck, while Father and Grumble stood by the end of the lowered tail ramp. Mother was staying at home, but she had provided a parting present for the Water Horse, a gift of food with which to lure him out of the lochan, up the ramp, and into the body of the truck.

There had been much discussion about what this lure should be. Chocolate chip cookies? Herring? Or the very first food that had ever passed Crusoe's infant lips — sardines?

"Trouble is," said Father, "that if I lay a trail of any of those, he's liable to find it difficult to pick them up off the ground. It'll slow him up and maybe he won't make the effort. What we need is something tasty that I can drag along in front of him, just out of his reach, something long enough to keep me clear of becoming an accidental meal myself."

"A string of sausages!" said Mother.

"A wonderful idea!" said Father. Now he paused a moment, looking and listening carefully, but he could see no one and hear nothing, so he walked to the brink and called "Crusoe!" and Crusoe came surging in.

Father and Grumble had feared that perhaps by now the Water Horse might be unwilling to leave the element in which, except for his move from goldfish pond to lochan, he had lived for over three years. But their fears were unfounded.

As Father walked slowly backward trailing the string of sausages, Crusoe, with an action like that of a giant caterpillar, humped himself out of the water and over the intervening ground toward the cattle truck. Up the slatted ramp he hauled himself, neck

outstretched in his effort to catch the end of the long sausage string, and into the body of the truck, while the springs creaked and groaned under his weight. Dropping the lure at the far end, Father nipped smartly out by the little side door, and ran around to the back. Then, as Crusoe was wolfing down the sausages with grunts of contentment, Father and Grumble each took hold of one side of the tail ramp and heaved it up and screwed the locking clamps tight. The Water Horse was loaded!

The journey itself was also uneventful. Southward they went at first to Glenfinnan, then due east along the north shore of Loch Eil, till they came to Fort William. They stopped by the banks of Loch Lochy. Father was a little worried that the Water Horse might become uncomfortably dried out, so here, at about the halfway mark of the journey, he and Grumble filled buckets and sloshed the contents through the slits in the side of the cattle truck. Crusoe bellowed quietly in appreciation.

By the side of Loch Oich they stopped again and repeated the operation. Kirstie and Angus got out to stretch their legs while Father and Grumble filled the buckets. Just as Father was about to toss in the last bucketful, they heard the noise of an approaching car.

"Off the road, children," said Father, for the way was narrow, and they all stood and waited for the vehicle to round the bend ahead. Tourists, they thought. But it was a police car. They watched as it came closer, willing it to go by without stopping, but it slowed and drew to a halt.

"Quickly," said Father to Grumble. "Lift the hood!"

A lone police officer got out of the police car. "Are you in trouble?" he asked.

Yes, we are, thought Father, but "No, we're not," he said in a cheerful voice. "Just going to top off the radiator. There's maybe a wee bit of a leak somewhere—she needs a drop of water now and again." He started to unscrew the radiator cap, gingerly, as though it were hot, and began to lift the bucket of water.

Fortunately, the policeman did not closely watch Father's attempts to fill an already full radiator, but turned to Grumble.

"Where are you bound?" he asked.

"Fort Augustus," said Grumble, truthfully. "A load of fat cattle for the slaughterhouse," he added, untruthfully.

"Your own stock?" asked the policeman.

"Oh, aye!" said Grumble, truthful once more.

"There's a good bit of rustling goes on in these parts, would you believe it?" said the policeman.

"Never!" said Grumble in an astonished voice.

"It's a fact," said the policeman. He looked at the old man and the two small children.

"Not that you're my idea of rustlers," he said, smiling. Then he put his eye to one of the slits in the side of the cattle truck.

Mercifully, he could see very little, for

Crusoe's bulk occupied all the available space, but he could just make out a great dark flank pressed against the truck's side. He poked it with a gloved finger, and Crusoe, thinking this to be a caress from his friends, gave a low bellow of pleasure.

"A fine big beastie that one seems to be," said the policeman. He turned to Angus.

"A good size, is it, laddie?" he asked.

"A monster," said Angus, solemnly.

The policeman laughed and ruffled Angus's hair as Father now joined them, having completed his pantomime with the radiator.

"Topped her off, have you?" said the policeman.

"Yes."

"Better get that leak seen to."

"Yes," said Father. "We must be getting along now."

"And so must I," said the policeman.

And, greatly to their relief, he did.

In the early afternoon they reached Fort Augustus, at the lower end of the great loch that they sought. A new road had recently been built along its northern shore, but Father chose the old southern road and drove steadily on, looking out all the while for a suitable place.

Just short of Dores, he found it. There was a rest area on the left, perched high above a steep bushy slope that fell directly into the loch. Here they stopped.

Crusoe himself did not exactly enjoy his journey. At first, when the tail ramp slammed shut on him, it felt strange for him to be confined. He was not afraid, for he did not know the meaning of fear, but he did not much care for the roar of the engine and the stink of gas fumes and the bumping and swaying motion of their progress. He started to feel a little sick.

After a while, however, he became used to things, and indeed, because it was the time of day when he always took his nap, he began to feel drowsy. He had almost

dropped off when the bumping and swaying stopped and some water was splashed
on him.

Nice giants, he thought to himself, and
gave a little bellow of thanks. Then it was
onward again, inside this strange cave in
which, because of his great size, he had
hardly room to move a muscle. A little
later, the bumping stopped again, more
water was thrown in, and Crusoe lowed in
appreciation as someone prodded his side.
But how cramped he felt, and what a relief
it was when at last the roaring and the jolt-
ing stopped for good, and the door behind
him swung down and let in the light.

Painfully, for his limbs were cramped,
Crusoe maneuvered himself backward and
down the slope of the ramp and to the
ground. And how pleasant it was to have
the old familiar tickling, for the two small
giants had each found a stick and enthusi-
astically went to work on him.

Then, as Crusoe squirmed pleasurably
around, he suddenly saw, beneath and

stretching away in either direction as far as the eye could see, an *enormous* expanse of water!

Get into it, every instinct told him, get under it. And he heaved his huge body to the edge of the rest area, and slithered over and crashed down through the bushes on the slope below, and fell with a mighty splash into the sun-dappled depths of the loch.

When he had gone, they all stood silently staring out over the still springtime waters.

Father felt pleasure and pride that the problem had been solved in a seamanlike manner.

Grumble felt relief that now at last the great beastie was in a safe place where he need worry about him no more.

Kirstie was remembering the time when Crusoe was only as long as the span of Grumble's hand. Fifty or sixty feet, Grumble had said he would grow to, and now she no longer doubted it.

Angus was remembering that he had forgotten to bring any emergency supplies.

For all of them, there was a sense of deep contentment that now the Water Horse had everything that he could want. Forevermore he would have the freedom of this great deep fish-filled loch, safe from all dangers.

He will be happy ever after, thought Kirstie, and because of that, so am I.

Father looked at his watch.

"My!" he said. "Will you look at the time! It's five to three already. We must be starting home or we'll be late for that high tea Mother is getting ready for us."

"Blow me down!" said Angus. "That would never do." And they clambered into the cattle truck and drove away.

Down, down, down the Water Horse dived, scattering great schools of fish as he went, down into the cold black depths, and then turned and shot upward, faster and faster, proud of his strength. For a moment all his training was forgotten, all the giants' teaching that he must not show himself unless summoned. He burst out into the sunshine in the middle of the loch and plunged and rolled around on the surface, so happy was he to be in this wonderful new watery world.

Then he came to his senses, and with a final great surge he sank from sight.

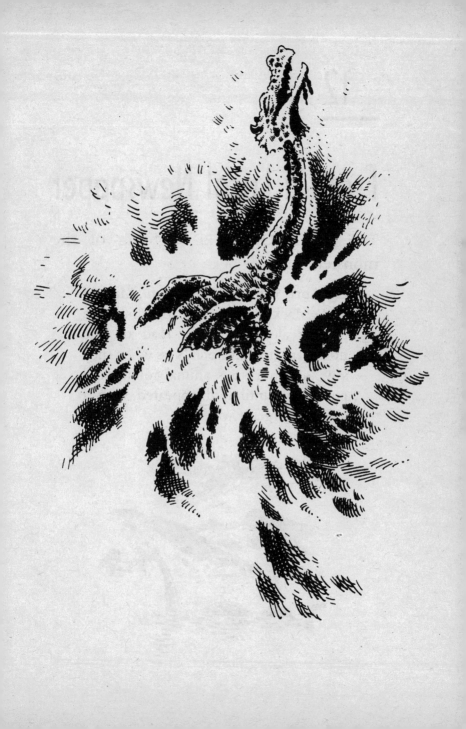

12

From a Local Newspaper

THE FIRST REPORTED sighting of the monster:

> On April 14th, 1933, at 3 p.m., Mr. and Mrs. Mackay of Drumnadrochit were driving along the new road on the northern shore of Loch Ness when they saw "an enormous animal rolling and plunging" until it disappeared with a great upsurge of water.

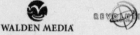